THE GRAND JOURNEY
OF MR. MAN

Canadian Cataloguing in Publication Data

Tibo, Gilles, 1951-
[Grand voyage de Monsieur. English]
The Grand Journey of Mr. Man

Translation of: Le grand voyage de Monsieur.

ENGLISH TEXT: SHEILA FISCHMAN.
For children.

ISBN 1-894363-64-7

I. Melanson, Luc II. Fischman, Sheila III. Title.
PS8589.I26G7313 2001 jC843'.54
C2001-900049-9
PZ7.T4333Gr 2001

Publisher: Dominique Payette
Series Editor: Lucie Papineau
Art direction and design: Primeau & Barey

Legal Deposit: 3rd Quarter 2001
Bibliothèque nationale du Québec
National Library of Canada

Dominique & Friends
Canada:
300 Arran Street, Saint-Lambert, Quebec,
Canada J4R 1K5

USA:
P.O. Box 800
Champlain, New York, 12919
Tel: 1 888 228-1498
Fax: 1 888 782-1481
E-mail: dominique.friends@editionsheritage.com

Printed in China
10 9 8 7 6 5 4 3 2

The publisher wishes to thank The Canada Council
for the Arts for its support, as well as SODEC
and Canadian Heritage.

Government of Quebec – Book Publication
Tax Credit Program – SODEC

THE GRAND JOURNEY
OF MR. MAN

For Lucie Papineau,
for the storied heart
G. T.

For my mother,
Laurence
L. M.

Story: Gilles Tibo
Illustrations: Luc Melanson
English Text: Sheila Fischman

After the death of his child,
Mr. Man left everything behind. He only held onto
his son's teddy bear and a chair to travel on.

At the train station, Mr. Man bought
a one-way ticket to anywhere.
He traveled on top of the last coach.

Some nights, depending
on where they had stopped,
Mr. Man would haunt
the playgrounds, humming
lullabies softer than
the breeze.

He visited the circuses. At the end of
every performance, after the crowds
had taken their laughter away,
Mr. Man would watch in silence
from the middle of the ring.

One day, the train stopped at the sea.
Lulled by the waves, Mr. Man gazed at sand
castles for a long, long time.

Then Mr. Man crossed the ocean on a liner.
Every evening at dusk he would join the passengers who
were watching the horizon fade away in the sky.

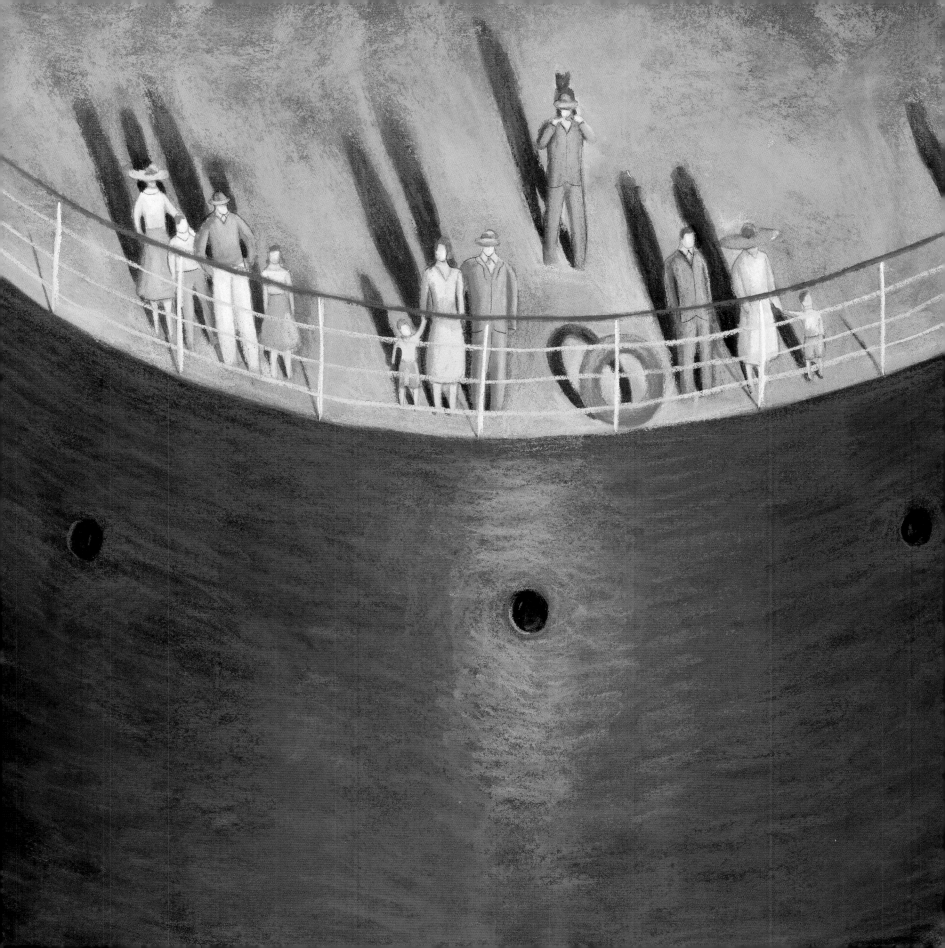

Mr. Man went around the world. In every town,
in every village, he would stroll up and down every street,
every lane and path.

Women and men invited him into
their houses. He would spend a few hours there,
just long enough to share a smile.

At the end of the world, Mr. Man
met a child. The boy's tears spoke of war
and the disappearance of his family.

For three days and three nights the child
cried over the ruins of his house. The only thing
that he found there was a rag doll.

Mr. Man unearthed a little wooden chair.

He repaired it and gave it to the child.

The little boy set his chair down next to Mr. Man's.
Together, they listened to the songs of
the birds and the sigh of the wind in the leaves.

Mr. Man lent the child his bear.
Stroking its woolly snout, the boy told
the story of the doll.

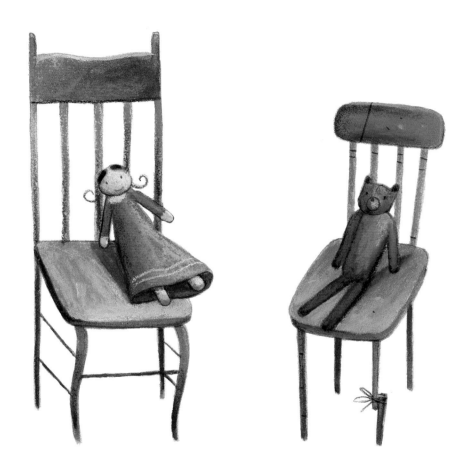

Since that day, the man and the child
have been traveling together, sitting side by side
and holding each other by the hand.